HENRY AND MUDGE
AND THE
Bedtime Thumps

The Ninth Book of Their Adventures

Story by Cynthia Rylant
Pictures by Suçie Stevenson

Ready-to-Read
Aladdin Paperbacks

To Patrick Perkowski, our good family friend—CR
For Harvey, Sophie, Luca, and Rose—SS

ALADDIN PAPERBACKS
An imprint of Simon & Schuster Children's Publishing Division
1230 Avenue of the Americas
New York, NY 10020

Text copyright © 1991 by Cynthia Rylant
Illustrations copyright © 1991 by Suçie Stevenson

THE HENRY AND MUDGE BOOKS
Also available in a Simon & Schuster Books for Young Readers Edition

The text of this book was set in 18 point Goudy
The illustrations are pen-and-ink watercolor

Manufactured in the United States of America
First Aladdin Paperbacks edition 1996

30 29 28 27 26 25

The Library of Congress has cataloged the hardcover edition as follows:
Rylant, Cynthia.
Henry and Mudge and the bedtime thumps:
the ninth book of their adventures / story by
Cynthia Rylant ; pictures by Suçie Stevenson.
p.   cm.
Summary: Henry worries about what will happen
to his big dog Mudge during their visit to his grandmother's house
in the country.
[1. Dogs—Fiction. 2. Grandmothers—Fiction.]
I. Stevenson, Suçie, ill. II. Title.
PZ7.R982Hes   1991
[E]—dc20   89-49529
CIP   AC
ISBN-13: 978-0-689-81011-4 (hc.)   [ISBN-10: 0-689-81011-3 (hc.)]
ISBN-13: 978-0-689-80162-4 (pbk.)   [ISBN-10: 0-689-80162-9 (pbk.)]
0310 LAK

Contents

To Grandmother's House

Henry and his big dog Mudge
were going to the country
with Henry's parents.
Henry was reading comic books.
Mudge was chewing his toenails.

They were going to visit
Henry's grandmother.
Henry's grandmother
had never met Mudge.
So Henry worried.
He worried that Mudge
might drool on her skirt.

He worried
that Mudge might
eat her coffee table.
But mostly he worried
that Mudge might
have to sleep outside.

Mudge had never
slept outside before.
And if Mudge slept outside,
Henry would be alone,
trying to sleep
in an empty room
in a strange house
in a dark yard
in the country.

Henry read his comic books
and worried.
The longer he rode,
the more he worried.
Soon he began
to bite his fingernails.

Chew, bite. *Spit.*
Chew, bite. *Spit.*
Henry bit his fingernails,
Mudge chewed his toenails,
and the car drove on.

"Hello, Sweetie"

After riding for a long time,
Henry and Mudge saw
the grandmother's house.
It had a birdbath
and a garden
full of corn.

Henry and Mudge
looked at each other.
Their fingernails
and toenails
were very short.

Henry's grandmother
came outside.
She had a big smile
and a polka-dot dress.
Mudge took one look
at her
and his tail wagged
and wagged
and wagged.

"Hello, sweetie,"
Henry's grandmother
said to Henry.
She hugged him tight.

"Hello, sweetie,"
Henry's grandmother
said to Mudge.
She hugged him tight.
Henry's grandmother wiped
dog drool off her sleeve,
and they followed
her into the house.

A Lot of Looks

Henry's grandmother's house
was very small.
It had a lot of tables,
and things on the tables.

Henry looked at Mudge,
and for the first time
wished that Mudge
was smaller.
Shorter.
Thinner.
Mudge looked like
an elephant in a
phone booth.

And before too long,
Mudge knocked
a pink flamingo
off of a table.
"Aw, Mudge," Henry said.

Henry's father
gave Mudge a look.

Then Mudge knocked
a wishing well
off of a table.
"Aw, Mudge," Henry said.

Henry's father
and Henry's mother
gave Mudge a look.

Then when Mudge knocked
a bowl of peppermints
off of a table,
Henry's father
and Henry's mother
and Henry's grandmother
gave Mudge a look.

And Henry's father said,
"Outside."

Mudge was put out.

Henry gave
everybody
a look.

The Bedtime
Thumps

After dinner,
Henry played outside
with Mudge.
They loved the birdbath,
Mudge especially.
It was like a
giant water dish
just for him.

When it was dark,
Henry's father
called Henry in.

"What about Mudge?"
asked Henry.
"He has to sleep outside,"
said Henry's father.
"*Outside?*" said Henry.

Henry looked at Mudge,
sitting in the dark
country yard.
Henry was afraid.
He was afraid
Mudge would be lonely.
He was afraid
Mudge would be sad.

But mostly he was afraid
Mudge would be asleep
if Henry needed
to be saved
from a bear

or a bobcat

or a giant moth

or a mouse.

Henry gave Mudge
a tight hug,
then he went inside,
biting his fingernails.
When he was washed
and in bed,
Henry lay in the dark.
His eyes were big.
His heart was pounding.
His knees were shaking.

Then

WISH! FLOP!

A moth!

Henry jumped
out of bed!
He ran to the
front door!
"Mudge!" he called out
in a loud whisper.

Thump.

Thump.

Thump.

Mudge wagged his tail
from under the porch table.

"Hi Mudge," Henry said
as he crawled under the table, too.
He was glad to see Mudge.
Mudge was glad to see him.

Mudge licked Henry's face
and smelled his ears
and shook his hand.

Then Henry laid his head
on Mudge's big chest,
and finally he slept
a good sleep
at the strange house
in the dark yard
in the country.

And when the moth
flew by,
Mudge ate it.